ISBN: 978-0-7358-4080-5 (trade edition)
9 11 13 15 · 14 12 10
Printed in Germany by Grafisches Centrum Cuno GmbH & Co. KG,
39240 Calbe, March 2013.

www.northsouth.com
www.nord-sued.com

The Elves of Cologne

Illustrated by Eve Tharlet · Translated by Anthea Bell

North South

They tell a tale in old Cologne
of little elves in days long gone,
when weary workers, should they please,
could laze about and take their ease.

And then by night –
oh, what a sight!
The little elves came chattering,
hustling, bustling, clattering.
They rubbed and they scrubbed,
they swept, washed and scurried,
they cleaned and they hurried
to finish the work,
and before you knew it
whatever there was to be done,
they'd do it!

The carpenter could sit down, yawning,
and sleep right through until next morning.
Meanwhile the helpful little elves
did all the building work themselves.
They took hatchet and saw
to window and door;
they hammered in nails,
built staircase and rails,
they slapped on plaster
like any master,
and then, for afters,
they fixed up the rafters.

And before the carpenter woke from his dreams,
the house was complete
with roof and beams!

The baker was a sleepyhead
and left the elves to bake his bread.
The baker's boy lay sleeping too.
The little elves knew what to do.
They strained their backs
hauling heavy sacks . . .

Weighed flour, mixed dough,
kneaded fast, kneaded slow,
let it rise to full size,
knocked it all down and put it to bake
before the baker was awake.
He and his boy were still lying down
when the loaves came out, fresh, crisp and brown.

The butcher took it easy too,
lost in his dreams the whole night through.
The little elves cut up the meat
and trimmed it too
all nice and neat.
They worked as fast
as the wind flies past.
They chopped and carved,
they quartered and halved,
they minced and rinsed,
stuffed the mixture in
the sausage skin . . .

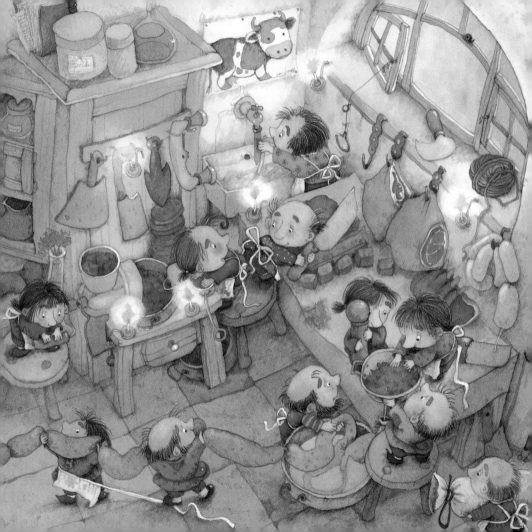

And when the butcher woke up next day
there were the sausages
on display!

The brewer in the tavern drank
until his head swam and he sank
dead to the world beside his cask.

The elves soon set about his task:
brewed beer and wine
both strong and fine.

They heaved and they hauled,
they hoisted, they called
to their friends to start tapping,
while the brewer lay napping,
to blend and to taste –
there was no time to waste!
And before the brewer
had stopped his snoring
his wine and beer
were ready
for pouring.

One day the tailor had to make
the Mayor a coat; it mustn't take
too long, so he laid down his head
beside his needles, pins and thread.
The elves came in
to tack and pin,
and cut and clip
and measure and snip,
and fit that coat
from hem to throat.

And before the tailor woke next day,
the coat was ready
to take away!

But the tailor's wife wanted to know
who had done all that work, and so
next night she scattered peas on the floor.

And when the elves
came through the door,
they staggered and fell
with a squeal and a yell.
They howled and they cried
as the peas made them slide.
They grumbled and stumbled
and downstairs they tumbled.

The tailor's wife came running down
to look, but in a flash –
they'd gone.

Alas, alas, and sad to say,
the elves no longer come today.

These days the craftsmen of Cologne
must do their work all on their own.
It keeps them all busy,
they get in a tizzy,
they bustle and scurry
and hasten and hurry,
they brew and bake,
they mend and make.
Oh, for the happy days of old!
But they are gone –
and my tale's told.